The Saltbox Sweater

Janet McNaughton

Tuckamore Books
a Creative Publishers imprint
St. John's, Newfoundland
2001

Le Conseil des Arts | The Canada Council
du Canada | for the Arts

We acknowledge the support of The Canada Council for the Arts
for publication assistance.

We acknowledge the financial support of the Government of
Canada through the Book Publishing Industry Development
Program (BPIDP) for our publishing actvities.

Cover Art and Design and illustrations © 2001, Nancy Keating

∞ Printed on acid-free paper

Published by
TUCKAMOREBOOKS
an imprint of Creative Book Publishing
A division of 10366 Newfoundland Limited
A Robinson-Blackmore Associated Company
P.O. Box 8660, St. John's, Newfoundland A1B 3T7

Printed in Canada by:
ROBINSON-BLACKMORE PRINTING & PUBLISHING

Canadian Cataloguing in Publication Data
McNaughton, Janet Elizabeth, 1953-
    The saltbox sweater

ISBN 1-894294-35-1

    I. Title

PS8575.N385S25 2001   jC813'.54   C2001-901093-1
PZ7.M33Sa 2001

for Nora

Chapter One

Katie woke to the growl of heavy equipment. On no, they'd started without her! She hurried into her clothes, then tore outside and up the hill. Mom and Nanny Grace were already there, and Uncle Len's family, their car packed for the mainland. With all the doors and windows pulled off, the cosy saltbox house that Katie's grandmother had lived in for so long already looked abandoned.

Katie's mother put her arms around Katie's shoulders and hugged. The backhoe pushed. The old house groaned and creaked until it sounded as if it were crying for help. Katie wanted to cover her ears. Just when she thought she couldn't stand it, a wall collapsed with a dusty sigh. Soon, the house was nothing but a heap of broken boards.

"Poor old house," Nanny Grace said. "Gone after almost two hundred years."

Uncle Len gave her a quick hug. "Now Mom," he said, "Don't cry. I couldn't bear to have the old house rot away. You know it's for the best. Tomorrow, the trucks will clear away this mess. Next summer, you'll have a nice big garden." He looked anxious to leave. "I'll call when we get to Alberta. You'll feel better once you're settled in with Celia and Katie."

Katie waved goodbye to her cousins, Bobby and Michelle, as Uncle Len's car disappeared. When they walked back down the hill, Nanny sighed. "This place seems empty," she said.

Katie looked around. Nanny was right. Quinter Cove was as pretty as ever. The harbour still nestled into the hills so perfectly, people called it the Teacup. Puffins still nested out on Bird Rock just as they always had. But Quinter Cove was not the same. Most people had lost their jobs when the fish plant in Avalon Station closed last year. Since then, half the families had left Newfoundland for the mainland. The empty houses gave Quinter Cove a sad, lonely feeling it had never had before.

"It wasn't like this when I was Katie's age," Nanny continued. "This place was full of life then. Boats were always coming and going. It seemed like everything was new. Only new thing around now is that big grocery store in Carbonear."

"And it's taking Mr. Verge's business," Katie's mom said. She glanced at her watch. "I'd better hurry if I want to keep my job."

Nanny Grace laughed. "Ed Verge won't fire you, Celia. You're the best worker he ever had."

"Well, I only got the job because the Porters moved," Katie's mother said.

Katie said nothing. Betty Porter had been her best friend. Now, she was just a pen pal. Katie's cousin, Michelle, had been the last girl in Quinter Cove in same grade as Katie in the school at Avalon Station.

And now she was gone. Katie had never been close to her cousin, but she knew she would miss Michelle.

"Don't look so gloomy, Katie," her mother said as she kissed her goodbye. "We're getting fresh strawberries in the store today."

"Then Katie and I will make shortcakes after we straighten things away," Nanny said.

Katie followed her grandmother into the house, remembering how frightened she had been when Uncle Len decided to move to Alberta a few months ago. Would Nanny go too? When Katie was little, Nanny had looked after her while Mom worked in the fish plant. Katie's father, Nanny youngest son, had died when his fishing boat went down in a storm at sea before Katie was even born.

Katie loved Nanny Grace as much as she loved her mother. But Nanny had always lived with Uncle Len's family in the saltbox house where she had raised her own sons. Nanny couldn't decide whether

to go or stay. The idea that she might leave with Uncle Len's family had kept Katie awake night after night.

Finally, one day, Nanny came to visit looking so serious, Katie was sure she had decided to go. "Len says I shouldn't be living alone," she began. "And maybe he's right. You know my heart's not perfect." Nanny paused. "They all want me to go with them." She didn't look happy.

Katie bit her lip, but said nothing.

"Is that what you want?" Katie's mother asked.

Katie's grandmother shook her head. "The more I think about it, the sadder it makes me. I've lived here all my life, Celia. If I had to leave now, I think I'd shrivel up and die."

"Well, you're welcome to live with us," Katie's mother said right away.

"Hurray," said Katie, throwing her arms around Nanny's waist. "This is the best news we've had in months." Mom and Nanny Grace had laughed.

So now, Katie's house was filled with all

the boxes and furniture Uncle Len brought down over the past few days. How would everything fit?

"Let's get to work, Katie," Nanny Grace said.

Katie took an old tin box from one of the cartons and opened it up. It was filled with old photos. She took one out. Nanny Grace looked over her shoulder. "That's your great-great grandparents on their wedding day," she said. "Grandfather Edwin made this daybed for Annie, his bride." Nanny pointed to the old couch. "It was in the old house ever since."

Katie took out another photo, this one of a solemn baby in frilly white clothes. Nanny Grace sighed. "All these children were born in that old saltbox house. Now the house is gone." Nanny dried her eyes.

"Show me what to do, Nanny," Katie said. Unpacking might keep Nanny's mind off the saltbox house.

They began to clear the cartons out of the living room, but Katie didn't put the old tin box of photos away. She left it on a table by the TV so she could look at the pictures later. All afternoon, while they worked, Katie pictured those Johnson babies, lined up on the daybed in frilly white clothes. She tried to make them smile, but they wouldn't. Not today.

By the end of the day the house was still cluttered, but it looked better. When Mom came home she carried a basket of fresh strawberries, but her face was grim. "Mr. Verge says he can't compete with that new store. Verge's is closing next month and I'll be out of a job," she said. "We should have gone with Len."

Chapter Two

Over the next few days, Katie's family talked about the future. Would they leave Quinter Cove? Mom thought maybe they should, but Katie and Nanny Grace had other ideas.

"We belong here," Katie said.

Nanny smiled. "That we do."

Mom ran her hands through her hair the way she did whenever she was worried. "Well, Employment Insurance will give us enough to live on for now."

"Don't forget my pension, Celia," Nanny Grace said.

Katie's mother smiled. "Thank you, Grace."

"So we can stay?" said Katie.

"Now, Katie, nothing's really settled.

Employment Insurance doesn't last for-
ever. If I don't find work, we'll still have to
think about leaving next year."

"Maybe the fish plant will reopen next
year," Katie said.

"No, Katie. The fish plant won't reopen
any time soon. I need to find new work."

A few weeks later, Mr. Verge closed the
store. When the shelves were almost
empty, he started to give away the things
he couldn't sell. "Anything take your fancy,
Katie?" he asked.

"Can I look in the loft?"

He nodded.

The loft of the old clapboard store was
gloomy and smelled of mothballs. Mr.
Verge had always let Katie and her friend
Betty Porter play up here under the low
roof beams on rainy summer days. Katie
loved the loft. It was filled with things no
one had ever bought—bright men's shirts
and old frilly dresses. But she was disap-
pointed as she looked around today. Playing dress-up was for little kids. There was
nothing here for her now. Just as she was

leaving, she saw three canvas bags tied to a ceiling beam, near the stairs at eye level. She lowered them, opened one and gasped with delight. Inside was wool in every colour of the rainbow. She ran downstairs. "Mr. Verge, can I have the wool?"

"Yes, child. Women stopped buying sheep's wool when they got that fancy acrylic yarn that doesn't shrink. I always liked real wool better myself. Take it and welcome."

Katie carried the bags home in three trips, singing all the way.

"What's this?" her mother cried. "You know the closets are all blocked up with

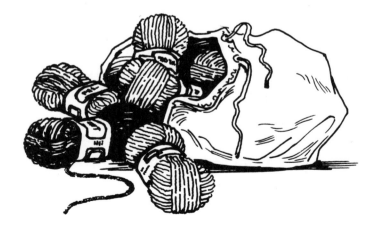

your Nanny's things. What were you thinking?"

These days, she always sounded angry. It's almost as if she's another person, Katie thought. "It's just wool," she said. Tears stung her eyes.

Mom noticed. "I'm sorry, Katie," she said, "Don't cry." She ran her hands through her hair. "Let's see if these bags will fit in the upstairs closet." The wool was put away, but the happy feeling it had given Katie was gone. It would be a long time before she wanted to see that wool again.

When Katie went downstairs, she found Nanny Grace sitting on the old daybed, looking up the hill where her house had stood. Katie got the box of old photos and sat down beside her. "Tell me about this one," she said, thrusting a photograph of a baby into Nanny's hands.

"This," she said, "is your Great Uncle Josiah Johnson. Your grandfather's oldest brother. He spent every summer of his life fishing on the Labrador from the time he was ten until he was sixty-eight. The summer after his father died, when he was just twenty-one, he took the schooner to Labrador himself with a crew of boys. They got caught in a snowstorm coming back to Quinter Cove in the fall. The ship was driven off course. It took them three weeks to find their way home, living on hard bread, salt cod and icicles they knocked from the rigging. Everyone had given them up for dead, everyone except Josiah's mother. She set a place for him at the table every night. When he finally showed up, three weeks late, she just said, 'Took your time getting home this year, my son,' and he said, 'Yes, mother, I did,' sat down to his supper, and that was that. "

Katie took the photo out into the garden. She looked at the little baby with his big, toothless grin, trying to picture him as a fearless grownup, knocking icicles off the rigging of his schooner to make his tea. But she could only imagine a little baby climbing the rigging. That made her giggle. She was still looking at the photo when a truck pulled up and Mr. Verge's son Lawrence got out.

"I'm going north to take a welding job for a year," he said, "My house will be shut while I'm gone. Dad thought maybe you could use this firewood. It will only rot it if stays outside my place." There was a big load of spruce logs in the back of his truck.

"I'll get Mom," Katie said.

When Katie's mother tried to pay Lawrence Verge, he laughed and waved her money away. "Sure, the wood was free when I cut it last winter," he said.

"This will keep down our heating costs," Katie heard her mother say to Nanny Grace.

For the rest of the summer, whenever Katie's mother seemed worried, she took a bucksaw outside and cut the spruce logs into woodstove-sized pieces. She came back into the house red-faced and sweating, but Katie noticed she always seemed happier.

Chapter Three

Now that Katie's mother had no job, going for the mail was an important part of the day. Mildred Parrot, the letter carrier, drove from Avalon Station to fill the mailboxes in Quinter Cove around eleven every morning, and Katie and her mother walked over just after to pick up the mail. The mailboxes were near the wharf. It was a lovely walk, down the crooked road to the Teacup. The fields of Quinter Cove were covered in wild roses and slender blue irises. The air was sweet with the smell of raspberry canes. Dragonflies snapped and whirred in the summer breeze that blew sweet and warm from the land on sunny days, or cool and salty from the sea when it was cloudy.

Halfway down the hill, Katie and her mother always stopped to check on the growing baby goats that the Button family were raising to sell to a dairy in Bonavista Bay. All summer, the young kids kept climbing the fence, or breaking it down. They ate cabbages and flowers out of people's gardens. One day, the little black one ate a tea towel off Mrs. Carter's back porch.

The kids always crowded around the fence to take dandelion greens from Katie,

bumping their heads under her hand for a scratch between the growing buds of their horns. Katie like the way their hair felt, rough and wiry. She counted them while they pushed and shoved around her. "...sixteen, seventeen, eighteen. They're all here today."

"I guess the tea towels of Quinter Cove can breathe easier," Katie's mother joked.

"They get into so much trouble," Katie said.

Her mother smiled. "Now you know why we call children kids."

As they reached the mailboxes, Katie looked out to the mouth of the harbour. She could almost picture Great Uncle Josiah Johnson's schooner sailing home from the Labrador. How could she be happy anywhere else?

Near the end of August, Katie's mother opened the mailbox to find a letter from the school board. "You didn't get yourself into trouble at school last year, did you?" she asked, opening the envelope. But Katie knew she was joking.

"Oh, this is interesting," her mother said, frowning a little.

Her tone of voice caught Katie's attention. "What does it say?"

"It seems there won't be enough children at the school to make a whole grade four class this year, so you're going together with the grade fives."

"Oh no!" said Katie.

"I know what you're thinking, Katie. Lots of people are worried the school might close in another year or two. But we'll just have to cross that bridge when we come to it."

"That isn't it," Katie said. As soon as the words were out of her mouth she wished them back. But it was too late.

"Well then, Miss, what's bothering you?"

Katie tried to think of a lie, but she never had been good at lying. So she was stuck with the truth. "I'll be in the same class as Kenny Burry."

"Oh," her mother said. "Cod-liver Ken." She struggled to keep a straight face, but burst out laughing. "Sorry, Katie," she said. "But sweetie, you should have forgotten that by now."

"Well, nobody else has. Any time people see Kenny Burry and me, *somebody* always has to tell how he put the cod liver down my back."

"It would have helped if you hadn't carried on the way you did. You screeched like someone was trying to murder you. People came running from all over the cove to find out what was wrong."

"I was just little. Anyway, I didn't know what it was." Katie shuddered even now. "It was so cold and slimy."

Katie's mother smiled as they started back up the hill. "I think we'd all have forgotten by now if Mr. Hand hadn't been on the wharf with his new video camera that day," she said.

Katie groaned. "Mr. Hand. He's always dragging people into his house to see the entire history of Quinter Cove since 1988 on video." After a minute she said, "Do you suppose the teacher will notice I never talk to Kenny Burry?"

"You don't? After all this time? Oh, Katie, that's silly."

Katie frowned. "No, it's not. I don't speak to Kenny Burry and I not going to start now, just because we're in the same class."

Her mother reached over and stroked Katie's hair. "Stubborn," she said, "Same as your father." And she got that far away look she always did when she spoke about Katie's father. Katie knew better than to try to talk to her mother when she looked like that.

Chapter Four

School started back and Katie's Mom still had no job. There just weren't any. Now, she stayed home all the time. This had never happened before. Would they have enough to eat this winter? Katie worried, but she didn't like to ask.

The weekend after Labour Day, there was a food fishery. All the boats went out on the bay. Everyone seemed happy to be busy. "Come on," Katie's mother said to her, "Let's see if this old knife still works." Katie knew her mother had been one of the best filleters in the fish plant. When there were competitions, she usually won. Once, she even went to St. John's to compete.

Mom went down to the wharf and stood by the old splitting table. When people landed their catch she filleted fish for them, just as she had at the plant. Anyone could see how happy she was to be working again. Lots of neighbours gave them cod. Nanny wrapped most of it up carefully and into the deep freeze it went. At least they'd have fish for winter.

Now, Katie had to get used to waiting for the school bus with no one her own age to talk to. No one except Kenny Burry, that is. Katie stole a glance at him now and again while they waited. He seemed like any other ten-year-old boy—a little messy, a little rough, not unpleasant or mean. But, after not talking to him for so long, Katie didn't know how to start. Kenny didn't seem to either, so they went on saying nothing, like always.

The only other kids who waited for the school bus were much younger. The littlest was Mrs. Carter's grandson. Katie didn't know him at all. He'd been born on the mainland while his father was in medical school. His parents had just moved back over the summer, and now his father was

working at the cottage hospital in Old Per-
lican.

The first day of school, the little boy's
mother dragged him down the hill, scream-
ing all the way. When the bus came, Katie
and another girl from up the shore had to
hold onto him until the bus pulled away.
"Mommy," he screamed, "Mommy, don't
go." But as soon as his mother was out of
sight, the little boy stopped crying. He
spent the rest of the ride looking quietly out
the window. The next morning, he
screamed and cried all over again.

After a few days, Katie decided to talk to
him. She sat down on the empty seat beside
him as soon as he stopped crying. "What's
your name?" Katie asked.

"Murphy," said the little boy.

It seemed like a strange name, but Katie didn't let that stop her. "Okay, Murphy,
why do you screech like that every day?"

He stuck out his lower lip. "Mommy
goes away."

"But you like school, don't you?"

Murphy nodded.

"I thought so. Mrs. Butler is the nicest teacher in the school."

Murphy smiled. "She's taking us to Carbonear to pick our pumpkin for Hallowe'en," he said.

Katie nodded. "We did too when I was in grade one."

All day, Katie thought about Murphy. She watched him at recess. He seemed happy with the other kids. By the end of the day, Katie had a plan. "Nanny," she said after supper, "Would you come to Mrs. Carter's with me?"

"Yes, my dear. But why?"

Katie told Nanny about the little boy who made such a racket at the bus stop every day. "I think I can help. I'd like to talk to Mrs. Carter first, but I don't want to go on my own."

"Just let me get my jacket," Nanny said.

Mrs. Carter's house smelled wonderful as she opened the door. "Gracie!" she cried. "Just in time for a slice of gingerbread."

Nanny smiled. "I imagine you know Katie, don't you, Elsie?"

"Of course. My dear, you're getting some big. What can I do for you?"

"It's about your grandson, Mrs. Carter," Katie began.

"That child! My Ellen has to pry the creature off her to go anywhere. If he'd been reared up here, he'd be a different boy, I can tell you that."

Katie didn't like the way Mrs. Carter talked about Murphy. She hadn't been sure how she felt about the little boy herself. Now, she wanted to protect him. "But he's happy at school," she said. "And he stops crying as soon as his mother's out of sight. That's what gave me my idea." And Katie explained what she wanted to do.

"That might just work," Mrs. Carter said when she finished. "You're right clever, you are. I'll tell my daughter, and you can try it out tomorrow morning."

"I hope Murphy doesn't mind," Katie said.

"Murphy! That child can't even say his own name. His name is Murray, after my husband, rest his soul. I suppose everyone at school thinks we named him Murphy, do they?" She didn't wait for Katie to answer. "Who in their right mind would give a child a name like that? People must think we're cracked. Now, have some gingerbread."

When Katie and her grandmother finally stepped outside again, Nanny had to hurry down the road so she could laugh without being heard. "Murphy! Sounds like one queer little stick to me."

"He's a perfectly nice little boy," Katie said.

"Well, I'd say Mrs. Carter and her daughter could use some help with him. This is good of you, Katie " Nanny said.

For the first time, Katie wondered why she was doing this. When she spoke again, she answered her own question. "I guess everyone who's left in Quinter Cove has helped us with firewood and fish and all. Maybe it's my turn to help out."

Nanny smiled in a way that made Katie feel warm all over.

The next morning, Katie didn't go right down to the bus stop. Instead, she marched

up the hill, past the empty lot where the old saltbox house had stood, until she came to a freshly-painted house. The little boy was waiting for her.

"Murphy," Katie said, "I've come to take you to the bus. Say goodbye to your mother." Katie tried to sound kindly but firm, like someone who didn't expect any nonsense.

Murphy's lower lip trembled but he said exactly what Katie told him to. "Goodbye, Mother." He sounded as if he never expected to see her again, but he put his hand in Katie's.

"Now," Katie said, "If we're quick, we'll have time to see what those goats are up to."

The goats were just as happy to see Murphy as he was to see them. The little boy never looked back up the hill towards his house. For the first time that fall, he boarded the bus quietly, just like everyone else.

Chapter Five

"How did you know Murray wouldn't cry if you took him to the bus?" Nanny asked on Saturday. Katie and her mother were helping Nanny take the vegetables in from her garden. They had pulled the carrots and cut cabbages. Now they were digging potatoes.

"I didn't. But I knew he didn't like it when his mother left him," Katie said, "I thought he might be happier if he left his mother instead."

Nanny smiled. "Well, it worked. Mrs. Carter phoned to say thank you. Her daughter would like to pay you something for taking Murray to the school bus every day."

Katie frowned. "I didn't do it for money. It's not a lot of trouble."

"I told her that, Katie, but going up and down the hill will get harder when the icy weather comes. Ellen is so relieved, she wants to make sure she doesn't have to go back to taking Murray to the bus herself again."

"How much do they want to pay, Grace?" Katie's mother asked.

"Fifty cents a day. Two-fifty a week."

"That's not much. Why don't you take it, Katie, just so they know they can rely on you?"

"If you think it's okay," Katie said. Her allowance was only a dollar a week now.

Katie helped collect the last of the potatoes. Soon all the work was done.

"I never had time for a garden," Katie's mother said. "I suppose that's changed. I'm glad you'll be here to show us what to do next spring, Grace. Now, who wants to drive into Carbonear?"

Katie smiled. She loved the drive to town, even if it was only for groceries. This

fall, everyone seemed to be having yard
sales. Katie's mother always stopped at
every one.

Today, at the first sale, Katie looked
around with new interest, thinking of the
extra money she'd be getting. By a table of
baby clothes, she found a box full of picture
frames. "How much are these," she asked
the woman.

"The picture frames? Oh, just a quarter
each."

Katie picked out two, a nice gold one,
and one that looked hand-carved.

"What are you going to do with those, Katie?" Nanny asked on the way back to the car.

"I want to frame some of the old baby pictures," Katie said. "We could hang them on the livingroom wall."

But when Katie got home, she found the pictures didn't fit. They fell out of the wooden frame, and sat crooked under the glass in the gold one. "I guess it wasn't a good idea after all," Katie said, putting the frames away.

The weather stayed sunny. Nanny and Mom picked berries just about every day. When Katie came home from school, the berries were picked, cleaned, and packed away in the deep freeze. Katie never saw a fresh berry all fall. "Couldn't we have blueberry muffins?" she asked one evening.

Her mother smiled. "This way, we'll have pies and muffins all winter."

Katie didn't say so, but she would have liked blueberry muffins now.

One day, Katie came home with a memo from school. "There's going to be a bake sale on Friday," she said, "To make money for library books. I want to make blueberry muffins."

"Well," Nanny said, "Just help yourself to the ones in the freezer."

Katie frowned. "Frozen blueberries make ugly muffins."

Katie's mother laughed. "She's right," she said. "Frozen blueberries dye the batter purple. The muffins look funny."

"Could you keep some out of the freezer for me tomorrow?" Katie said. "Nobody will buy ugly muffins, no matter how good they taste."

"We will," Katie's mother promised.

But when Katie came home from school the next day, there were no berries in sight. "Where are my blueberries?" Katie asked.

"Your blueberries? Oh, the muffins! Katie, I'm sorry. We're so used to putting all the berries away, I just forgot."

Katie sighed. "I'll pick some myself. Is there anywhere you haven't already picked over?"

"We haven't been out by Church Pond

path yet," Katie's mother said. "The berries are usually good up there. Make sure you're back before supper."

Katie picked up an empty salt meat bucket as she left the house. She found the path by the white clapboard church, almost hidden by stand of spruce trees. Past the old graveyard, the trees thinned out. Katie picked a few blueberries as she walked up the grassy path, but not many. The berries grew thickest near the pond. As the path climbed, she could look down at all of Quinter Cove. It was so pretty, Katie wondered why she didn't come here more often.

When she was almost in sight of the pond, Katie saw something strange ahead. It looked like a piece of raw chicken on a rock. It made her skin crawl. Suddenly, a small, sharp-faced animal popped up from behind the rock. Katie dropped her berry bucket and screamed. The animal disappeared.

"What'd you have to go screeching for?" a voice cried from the bush on the other side of the path. "I finally get that mink lined up for a shot, and you screech your head off." It was Kenny Burry.

Katie felt herself turn bright red. "Why'd you want to blow the head off some mink anyway?" she said. "You could have killed me." Then she noticed the camera around Kenny's neck. "Oh," she said.

Kenny grinned. "Guns aren't the only thing that shoot," he said, "But that would have been my first guess too. My uncle's a photographer in Carbonear. He bet me five dollars I couldn't get a good shot of that mink last May. Been at it ever since." He sighed. "I was that close."

"Sorry," Katie said. "The chicken looked creepy, and the mink scared me."

"Well, I guess that makes us even for the cod liver." Kenny grinned again.

"I don't see how," Katie said. "I yelled myself silly both times."

Kenny shrugged. "That mink won't be back today. I'm going to have a mug up by the pond. Like some roasted chicken?"

Katie looked at the chicken thigh on the rock. It wasn't very clean. "No thanks," she said. But she didn't want to sound un-friendly. "I'd have some tea though."

"Hot chocolate," Kenny said. "I've only got one mug, but that's okay. We can share." He handed Katie her berry bucket.

Katie picked berries while Kenny made a fire on the rocks by the pond. When she was finished, he gave her the mug. "You have it," he said, "Chicken and chocolate probably don't go together." After an awkward silence, Kenny spoke again. "I liked what you did for that little fella, Murphy."

Katie didn't say anything, but she smiled down into the cup of hot chocolate. From now on, it would be easy to talk to Kenny.

Chapter Six

Everyone was surprised when Mr. Verge won a license to hunt moose, and even more surprised when he bagged his moose just a few weeks later. "There's moose enough to feed four families," he said to Katie's mom. "I thought at least Lawrence and his wife would be here, but now there's just me. You have to help me out." Katie's family helped him out by filling the deep freeze with moose roasts and moose steaks and ground moose and stewing meat. Katie wasn't worried about food any more.

But now, the berries were gone and the sunny days seemed to go with them. Day after day it rained until Katie almost forgot what blue sky looked like. Nanny bought paint and wallpaper on sale in Carbonear.

Mom and Nanny painted and papered every room in the house. Katie got used to walking around ladders and buckets. The mess was awful, but it kept Mom and Nanny busy.

By the time the wet weather turned cold, the freezer was full. Everything was papered and painted. There didn't seem to be anything left for Mom to do. Nanny's soap opera didn't interest Mom at all.

One night, Katie's mother said, "Grace, we've got all that wool upstairs. Why don't you teach me to knit?" They pulled Katie's wool from the closet. Nanny smiled when she saw the beautiful colours. "I'll get my knitting needles."

Katie's mother made a scarf. Nanny Grace said, "You learn fast Celia. Let's try something a little harder." Katie's mother made a stocking. She worked at it steadily, but it took days. Sometimes, she made mistakes. Then she had to pull the stitches out and start again. But Nanny praised her. "This is good, Celia. See how neat and even the stitches are, Katie? Your mother's

got a knack for knitting. Let's try two colours." Katie's mother learned to change colours and follow a pattern. Now the knitting needles flashed just like Mom's filleting knife used to in the fish plant. She hummed while she worked.

Every few days, Katie found a new stocking when she came home from school. But she noticed something. "Those socks don't match, Mom," she said.

Mom smiled."That's okay." Soon, stockings were everywhere. No two were alike. What was she doing?

One day in November, Nanny was waiting for Katie when she came home from school. "I was over to Mrs. Carter's for tea this afternoon," she said, "A few of the other ladies were there as well. They were saying how lucky I am to have a granddaughter at home. Most of their children are on the mainland now. We talked about what a sad Christmas this will be. Most families can't afford to come home for the holidays.

"Then we started talking about the way Christmas used to be. That gave us an idea. We thought we might put on an old fashioned Christmas concert in the community centre, just like we did in the old days when it was the school."

Katie poured herself a glass of milk. "But we don't have enough kids for a real concert," she said.

Nanny nodded. "We talked about that too. Some of us older folks could do recitations and songs. We want to have a bake sale and a craft table too. We'll use the money to fix the swings by the swimming hole." Nanny's eyes were glowing in a way Katie hadn't seen for a long, long time.

"I think that's a great idea," Katie said.

"Wonderful," Nanny said. "This will be some fun."

A wet snow was falling when Katie and her grandmother walked down the hill to the community centre for the first rehearsal a week later. It was only four o'clock, but it was almost dark. They passed the empty pasture where the goats had played all summer. They were gone to the dairy farm now.

It made Katie shiver to think of the long winter ahead. The darkness deepened. When they reached the community hall, Katie looked back up the hill. Some houses already had their Christmas lights on. They reflected on the water like coloured stars in a deep, black sky. Somehow, they made Katie feel warm again.

But inside the community centre, everyone kept their coats on. It was so cold that Katie could see her breath.

"I'll boil the kettle," Nanny said. "I'm sure there's one in the kitchen."

"We'd be fine if we had a fire in the woodstove," Mr. Hand said.

"We'll just have to do what we did back when this was the school," Mr. Verge replied.

Mr. Hand laughed. "You mean, bring our own firewood?"

"That's a good idea," Mrs. Carter said, rubbing her hands together. "Who lives closest?"

Kenny Burry put up his hand.

"Run home and get us a good armload of firewood for today, Kenny, please?"

Kenny nodded. As he left, Mr. Verge said, "Next week, everyone can carry a junk of wood to rehearsal." He smiled. "Just like the old days."

While Kenny got the fire going, everyone sat down around the stove with mugs of hot chocolate and tea to talk about the concert, all except for the smaller children, who played with some old Christmas decorations Mr. Hand found in a cupboard. "We could use a piano," Mrs. Carter said.

"Sure, we don't need a piano. I've got my karioke machine," Mr. Hand said. "With a special Christmas tape."

Mrs. Carter wrinkled her nose. "That's not very traditional."

"Elsie," Mr. Hand said, "You've got to move with the times. It's either that, or move the whole show into the church and use the organ."

Everyone groaned. The church needed a new organ. The keys were always sticking, giving the music unexpected long notes.

The room was almost comfortable by the time the meeting was over. "That settles it then," Mr. Hand said. "We'll meet again next Tuesday to get to work. The little ones can sing 'Away in a Manger.'" The older children will sing 'Joy to the World,' and 'Angels We Have Heard on High.'" All the children will lead the sing-a-long. The older folks will do 'Christmas in the Trenches,' and 'All I Want for Christmas is my Two Front Teeth.'"

"I think we need one more piece from the children," Nanny said. "I'd like to hear 'T'was the Night Before Christmas.' Katie, I think Murray could do a good job on that, don't you?"

Before Katie could speak, Mrs. Carter said, "Grace, you must be joking. That child is useless."

Katie glanced at Murphy, playing tag with the other children. He hadn't heard, but it made Katie mad to think Mrs. Carter would talk about her own grandson that way. So she pushed aside any doubts she had about Murphy herself. "I'm sure he could, Nanny. I'll help him." Katie smiled. They would show Mrs. Carter.

Later, as they walked home, Katie said, "Did you really have to carry your own firewood to school?"

"I'm surprised you never heard about that," Nanny said. "That old school was something else. After supper, I'll tell you all about it."

Chapter Seven

Soon, the concert was the most important event in the Quinter Cove Christmas calendar. No one was allowed to watch the rehearsals. Katie was afraid Mom would feel left out when she and Nanny left twice a week after school with their firewood. But Mom just waved her knitting needles at them as they left. The pile of odd stockings beside her chair grew bigger and bigger. Katie began to worry. Maybe being unemployed wasn't healthy for her mother. She tried to talk to Nanny about it on the way to rehearsal one day. "Don't you think all those odd socks are...a bit strange?"

Nanny only laughed. "Your mother's happy when she's knitting, Katie. I think she knows what she's doing."

Everyone wanted the Christmas concert to be special, but it was harder than Katie had imagined. Mr. Hand's karioke machine didn't work out. When the children tried to sing along with the tape, their voices were all fuzzy and distorted. Even the Christmas tape sounded wrong. "Too much percussion," Mr. Verge finally said one day. "This just isn't working."

Everyone agreed, except Mr. Hand. Katie could see him struggling to keep his good nature. "Well," he said after a long silence, "We could move into the church and use the organ."

"That organ is worse than ever," Nanny said. She turned to Mr. Verge. "Ed, suppose you play your accordion for the children."

Mr. Verge shook his head, but slowly, as if he was thinking. "I don't know what to say, Grace. I haven't touched it since Irene died. Didn't ever plan to pick it up again, to tell the truth."

Granny didn't push him. "Maybe the children can sing alone."

So they tried. But even from the middle

of the choir, Katie knew their voices sounded thin and small.

"Our singing isn't going to cheer anybody up," Katie told Nanny on the way home.

"Give Mr. Verge some time to think, Katie," was all Nanny said.

Between rehearsals, Katie climbed the hill to Murphy's house to help him learn the poem. For someone too little to read, he learned fast. Katie was sure he was going to impress everyone. Even Mrs. Carter.

"Murray, that's wonderful," Murphy's mother said one night when he finished with no mistakes. "Katie, you've done a great job."

Murphy's father spoke from behind his paper. "Maybe your mother will notice," he said. Murphy's mother frowned but she didn't say anything.

As the concert approached, Katie watched to see if Mr. Verge would bring his accordion to rehearsal, but he didn't. For once, Nanny was wrong.

The afternoon of the concert, everyone

The afternoon of the concert, everyone helped decorate the hall. Then came the dress rehearsal. Katie still thought the choirs sounded too small, but when Murphy did his poem, it was perfect. Everyone clapped at the end.

"Well," said Mrs. Carter, "That was lovely, Murray, my son." For the first time, Katie felt a warm place in her heart for Murphy's grandmother.

Katie was too nervous to eat supper. On top of everything else, her mother was acting strange. Even Nanny noticed. "You look like the cat that swallowed the canary, Celia," she said.

"Maybe I am," Katie's mother replied. "Run along now and get ready, both of you," she said. "I'll clear the dishes away and see you at the hall."

By the time Katie got to the community hall, the butterflies in her stomach were turning cartwheels. She wanted to run away. But Katie gasped as she stepped inside. Two fresh-cut trees stood on either side of the stage, decorated with lights and

tinsel. The hall was filled with the scent of fir and lit with the lovely, low light of the Christmas trees. "Oh, Nanny," Katie said, "Who did that?"

Nanny smiled. "Mr. Verge and Mr. Hand wanted to give you youngsters a present for all the hard work you've done the past few weeks. Let's see if they need help with the craft table."

Kenny Burry was already busy at the craft table, laying something out. In the low light, Katie thought they were flat sheets of glass, but then she realized they were framed photographs. She picked one up. The surprised face of a mink stared back at her. "You got your mink!"she said.

"I did. Just a week or so after you scared her away. My uncle gave me the five dollars he bet me. Then he showed me how to frame my work. He says I'll need to know how if I'm going to be a photographer."

Katie heard the pride in Kenny's voice. She noticed how neatly the framed the photos were. How did he do that? she wondered, remembering her try at framing the Johnson babies. But there wasn't time to ask. People were arriving. Katie hurried backstage to help get the little ones ready for 'Away in a Manger.' She heard Mr. Verge say, "Put that chair out on the stage, Kenny, just to one side." Katie noticed the small black case in his hand.

When the children were on stage, Mr. Verge took out his button accordion. He played an introduction, and the little kids began to sing. The accordion music seemed to carry their small voices out across the hall. They sounded wonderful.

When Katie's choir sang, she looked at the audience. The full hall had never seemed so empty. She could have named every person who was missing. But then she noticed her mother. She still looked happier than Katie could explain, and she carried a big canvas bag. What was she up to?

Mr. Verge's accordion was a hit at the sing-a-long. People even step danced in the aisles. Then, finally, it was Murphy's turn. Katie watched from the side of the stage while his grandmother led him to middle, parted the curtain and placed him before the audience.

Murphy had been fine singing with the other children. But now, alone, he froze and covered his face with his hands. After a painfully long pause, Katie heard Mrs. Carter hiss, "Murray, what's wrong?" Murphy didn't move, not even when his grandmother nudged him from behind the curtain. Katie looked around, unsure. Mr.

Verge caught her eye and nodded. "Out you go," he whispered.

Katie found herself in the centre of the stage, alone with Murphy. He was right. It was scary. She didn't think she could get him to move, so she put her arm around his shoulder and said, "Murray learned a poem and he'd like to say it for you now, wouldn't you Murray?" Murphy kept his hands over his eyes. Katie took a deep breath. After all these weeks of helping him, she was almost sure she could get through the poem alone. Almost.

"T'was the night before Christmas..." she began. It wasn't until the third verse, "When out on the lawn there arose such a clatter..."that Katie heard Murphy's voice through his fingers. By the time "a little old driver, so lively and quick" appeared, Murphy's hands were by his sides and he was reciting in a clear, strong voice. When Katie forgot a line near the end, Murphy helped her. When they said, "Happy Christmas to all, and to all a good night," the crowd burst into wild applause. People jumped to their feet.

"You just about brought the house down," Mr. Hand said, stepping past them as they left the stage. "Ladies and gentlemen, that's the end of our concert. There's tea and coffee and a bake sale and craft table at the back of the room..."

"Wait!" someone cried. Katie froze. It was her mother's voice. "Wait," she said again, and she rushed onto the stage. What was Mom doing? She opened the big canvas bag. Suddenly, she looked shy, as if she'd just realized where she was. "I made stockings," she said. "One for every boy and girl in Quinter Cove." She pulled one out and held it up.

Nanny and Mr. Verge quickly gathered the children. Every kid got a Christmas stocking, even Katie. No two were alike. Everyone left the concert smiling.

Chapter Eight

All January it rained and snowed. There were still no jobs. Will we have to move this summer? Katie wondered, but she didn't ask. Asking might make it happen. Now that the Christmas stockings were finished, Katie's mother didn't seem to know what to do with herself. It was going to be a long, dreary winter.

Then, one night, while Katie was doing her homework at the kitchen table, a knock came to the door. Katie peered past her mother's shoulder to see a strange woman. "Can I come in?" she asked. Katie's mother moved aside. "My name is Anne McGrath. I work for the Crafts Development Association. I'm out here visiting some crafts workers.

"Everywhere I went today, people showed me your Christmas stockings," she said, "I love what you do with colours. You have talent. Have you ever thought about taking craft courses in St. John's?"

"I like to, but I have no place to stay in St. John's. We can't afford it."

By now, Nanny Grace was in the kitchen too. She frowned at Katie's mother's words, but didn't contradict her. Even Katie knew it was true.

"That's too bad. I think you should learn to make sweaters."

Nanny Grace smiled. "That's a good idea, Celia. I could teach you."

"I'll lend you design books," Ms McGrath said, "If your sweaters are as interesting as those stockings, you could submit your work for the Christmas craft fair next November."

"Next November? That's a long time." Katie's mother sighed. "I'll try sweaters, Ms McGrath, but we'll have to move by the end of the summer if I don't make money."

Nanny taught Katie's mother how to

make sweaters. Once again, the knitting needles flashed and she hummed while she worked. Before the winter was over, she knew how make her own designs. Her sweaters weren't like anyone else's. Knitted puffins flew over Bird Rock. Her knitted blueberries looked ready to pick.

"These sweaters are special," Nanny said one evening. Katie thought so too. As the snow melted, they got Kenny to take photographs of the sweaters and sent them to Ms McGrath.

The puffins returned to Bird Rock. New baby goats came to the pasture. Katie's family waited and waited, but there was no word from Ms McGrath. One day, Katie found Nanny Grace staring out the window, up the hill where the saltbox house had stood.

Katie went for the box of old photos. "Tell me about this one," she said.

Nanny smiled at the photo of a little, frowning baby. "Now this," she said, "was Nancy Johnson, born Nancy Emberley. My mother-in-law, and your great grandmother. She's the one told me all the stories about the babies and what they grew up to be. And she learned from her mother-in-law, Annie. Quite the storyteller, Annie was. Spent her whole life in Quinter Cove, never went farther than Carbonear, but she knew everything that ever happened in this place."

"Like Mr. Hand," Katie said.

"Yes, like Mr. Hand. Now let's see what else I can tell you," Nanny said. Katie was beginning to feel that every baby in every photograph was her friend.

Summer came, and there was still no letter from Ms McGrath. One day, Katie's mother said, "My sweaters must be too unusual." She folded the sweaters into the canvas bags and put them away.

Katie felt a lump in her throat. I don't want to be the last Johnson to leave Quinter Cove, she thought.

That night, Katie dreamed about Verge's store. But instead of groceries, sweaters filled the shelves. Katie knew what to do. After school, she went to Mr. Verge.

"Mr. Verge, could we borrow your store for the summer?"

He laughed, but when Katie explained, Mr. Verge stopped laughing. "Let's talk to your mother," he said.

"But Mr. Verge," Katie's mother said, "I can't pay rent."

"I don't need rent, Celia. Just pay the electric bill. You could sell other people's crafts too."

Katie's mother bit her lip. "Well," she said finally, "it might be a start."

"Hurray," Katie said.

Her mother smiled, but said, "Don't get your hopes up, Katie. If the sweaters don't sell and I don't get into the Christmas craft fair, we'll have to leave."

They called the store "Quinter Cove Crafts." They sold Mr. Hand's wooden whirligigs and Mrs. Carter's rag dolls too. Katie worked in the store whenever she could.

"Why don't you play outside?" her mother would say.

"I like it here," said Katie. She dusted shelves and folded sweaters. On windy days, she put the whirligigs outside. They chattered in the wind like kittiwakes. Money trickled in. Enough money? Katie couldn't ask. She still watched for a letter from Ms MaGrath.

One day, Kenny came to the store with a box in his arms. "Could I sell my photos, do you think?" he asked Katie's mother.

Katie's mother opened the box. "Oh, Kenny, they look so professional. Of course you can. Where should we put them?"

"Out of the sunlight," Kenny said. "It fades them. How about over here? I brought a hammer and some picture hangers."

While Katie watched Kenny work, she thought about the old baby pictures again. "How do you do that?" she asked.

"You just pound the nail into the wall," Kenny said.

Katie laughed. "Not that. How do you frame the pictures?"

"Oh, that. It's not hard when someone teaches you. Why?"

"We have all these old photographs. Nanny tells me stories about the people in them. But none of them are framed."

"Why don't you give them to me?" Kenny said. "I think old photos need special mats. But my uncle would know. He's coming over tonight."

Katie smiled. "That would be great." Katie ran to get the photos. When Kenny saw them, he frowned. "These are all just babies."

"They're not *just* babies," Katie said, and she began to tell Kenny some of the stories that Nanny had told her.

When she finished, Kenny took the photos. "I'll see what Uncle Mark can do," he said.

For the first time, Katie wondered about money. "Will it cost much?"

Kenny shook his head. "Your mother didn't ask for money when she took my

work. My uncle says most people take a percentage."

Nanny Grace and Mrs. Carter started a tearoom in the store. Mrs. Carter's gingerbread brought more people. A reporter wrote about the store in the local newspaper. More tourists came. Katie helped out in the tearoom when it got busy. Even Murphy came sometimes.

"Murphy," Katie said one day, "Could you put these dishes in the sink?"

Murphy took the dishes, but he said, "My name is Murray."

Mrs. Carter smiled. "Yes, my son. Murray is so your name." And she patted him on the head. Katie realized she hadn't heard Mrs. Carter say one mean thing about Murphy since the Christmas concert. I'd better remember to call him Murray, she thought.

Kenny brought the photographs back a few days later. Katie hardly recognized them. "They look wonderful," she said.

Kenny blushed with pride. "My uncle found these old frames in St. John's. I got picture hangers too. Let's put 'em up."

When Nanny and Mom came home from the store that night, Katie showed them the photos. Eight little babies in frilly white dresses peered out from their frames beside the window above the old daybed.

Nanny hugged Katie. She didn't say anything, but Katie knew how happy she was.

Everyone thought the store was a real success. Katie's mother was working on a new design, but she kept it hidden. "This one's a surprise," she said.

One Saturday, they sold nine sweaters. "Does this mean we can stay?" Katie asked as they counted the money at the end of the day.

Her mother sighed. "Soon, the tourists will be gone. We can't get through the winter without the Christmas craft fair. I've been writing to your Uncle Len. He'll start to look for a place for us as soon as I say the word."

On the way home, Katie scowled at the mailboxes. Everyone liked Mom's sweaters. Why didn't Ms MaGrath write?

Next weekend was rainy. The tourists stayed away. All this work, Katie thought, just to end up living in some city full of strangers. She hardly noticed the car stopping.

"Oh, hello," Katie's mother said. Katie looked up. It was Ms MaGrath.

"I was away taking courses. No one opened my mail while I was gone. We love your sweaters! We want you to enter the

"Best New Product" category at the Christmas craft fair. Do you have any new designs?"

Katie's mother smiled. "This was a secret but..." She opened her bag. There, on the half-finished sweater, was Nanny's saltbox house.

"This is special," Ms MaGrath said.

"Yes it is," said Nanny Grace. Katie pretended not to see the tears. They were happy tears.

After supper, Katie and her mother walked out along the landwash to look at Bird Rock. "This means we can stay, doesn't it?" Katie asked.

"If you're sure that's what you want, Katie. It will be a struggle, you know that, don't you?"

Katie nodded. "That's okay," she said, "I'd miss everyone if we went away. Even Mrs. Carter. As long as we're in Quinter Cove, I can picture all the things that happened in the stories Nanny tells me. I can't imagine living anywhere else. I think I'd even miss the goats."

Katie's mother laughed.

That night, as Katie fell asleep, she saw all the Johnson babies in frilly white clothes. But they weren't in their picture frames. Instead, they were lined up on Great-Great Grandfather Edwin's daybed all together.

Every one looked happy. Every one smiled a big, toothless smile.

A Note About This Story

Fishing always played an important role in Newfoundland and cod was always the most important fish. This suddenly changed in the early 1990s when the government of Canada realized the cod stocks were disappearing. Not everyone agrees on the reasons why this happened, but overfishing by big factory freezer ships played an important role.

In July of 1992, the northern cod fishery was completely shut down. This was called the Moratorium. Over the next few years, fish plants across the Island closed and about 8,000 people left the province for other parts of Canada. Many of them were leaving places where their families had lived for generations. Many of them did not want to go. Some people managed to find new ways to earn a living in their home communities and some fish plant workers, like Katie's mother, retrained to become craft workers.